BABY IS A THING BL

A collection of flash fiction
by *Keely O'Shaughnessy*

abuddhapress@yahoo.com

For Andy

ISBN: 9798834330554

These stories have been previously published in anthologies and magazines:

"What If We Breathed Through Our Skin?"- *Legerdemain
The 2021 National Flash Fiction Day Anthology*, June 21

"The God, the Baby and the Lichtenberg Figure"- *The Drabble*, June 21

"She Will Recover Her Wings"- *Retreat West* Monthly Micro contest, April 21

"Thorns Are Meant to Prick the Heart of Sinners"- *Ghost Orchid Press*, November 21

"The Locked Cupboard"- *Reflex Fiction*, September 21

"Friday Night at the Cinema"- *Pretty Owl Poetry*, Spring 20

"Teaching a Clean Front Kick"- *Snow Crow* (8th Bath Flash Fiction Award anthology),
December 21

"Hidden in the Margins of a Gideon's Bible"- *Versification*, September 21

"The Depth at Which Spider Crabs are Found"- *No Deer Magazine*, April 21

"Floatation Therapy" - *Complete Sentence*, July 21

"The Space Between Where We've Been and Where We Are is Saltwater"-
Emerge Literary Journal, September 21

"The Manicure"- *Five on the Fifth* October 21

"Echoed Back"- *Idle Ink*, November 21

"The Asarco Smokestack '93" - *(mac)ro(mic)*, November 21

"Loss Is Riding the Log Flume at Splash Town in Late Summer" - *Cotton Xenomorph*,
July 22

"The Secret to a Maze is to Keep Turning Left"- *Retreat West* (monthly micro contest
first prize), May 22

"Moon swimming and Monster Hunting" *The Swell of Seafoam- Ghost City Press*,
Summer Series, July 22

"Practising Tricks, Spells, and Other Incantations" - *Selcouth Station Press, November
21*

Contents

Baby is a Thing Best Whispered

Before the rehearsal dinner, I learnt that only thirty hours after conception a fertilized egg begins to divide and starts to grow, and I thought I could sense the swelling of my shape right then, the quickening of life within me.

Disabled girls aren't supposed to be married or be mothers. They're meant to fade into dirt like leaf mulch. Yet here I am wearing an off-white dress and drinking fizzy grape juice from a champagne flute. The pearl of life in my belly only the size of a mustard seed.

Standing on the dance floor, I'm conscious of my chicken-scratch legs beneath the tulle of my skirt. The tight knotted mess of them against the newly gained curve of my bump, which nobody seems to notice. Coloured lights pulse. "Friday I'm in Love" plays as a side seam pops.

My husband doesn't know I'm pregnant. We were too busy drawing up seating plans and taste testing menus. He didn't notice when I declined the Bordeaux that was paired with the spring lamb option.

I whispered the word baby to my seamstress during my second fitting, as she worked on her knees, pinning up the hem. I worried about the bodice corseted tight against my newly stretched flesh. She loosened the binding and zipped her lips with her finger. No squeals of excitement or gentle congratulatory hugs. I knew what she was thinking, because it was my thought too. If I cannot give the cluster of cells embedded in the lining of my womb the right nourishment, my child will not survive.

~

The speeches were long and winding, and I didn't feature much. My mother is proud that I've found someone to care for me before my body parts seize completely.

She's dancing now, throwing slow, bluesy shapes across the dance floor. An old friend of the family swirls about beside her. I don't know if the friend is the same one that soothed her as she wept for the stillborn child that came before me. I was the consolation prize. When

Mum was sliced open, I had already been starved of oxygen.

Suffocating and too small, my brain was damaged. This is a detail that

is unsaid but remains nestled in the dark of my mother's throat.

She notices me and continues to move with a freedom I can only

imagine. With a practiced look she warns me to stand taller: act more

normal. A reflex, I stretch, my spine uncurling like a fern's frond.

Backlit by the DJ booth, my silhouette looks engorged.

At three weeks, a pre-born child's heart is almost fully formed. Their

eyes defined shapes, and their brain, spinal column, and nervous system

virtually complete. At twelve weeks, there is a clear heartbeat. Hands

pressed to my stomach, I sense a thrumming rhythm from within.

Something forcing its way out of the dirt. Eyes closed, I feel my bump

growing, organs shifting, fabric and flesh straining, and I know this is

happening too fast.

Someone elbows me, my husband's colleague, perhaps. He's drunk,

eyes blurred; my dress and veil spark nothing in him. I want to leave, but instead I'm pushed to the epicentre, helpless against the tide of swaying figures.

Looking down at my body, I'm startled by the new heft of it. And as more seams tear, I see there's a rupture in me. Spilt flesh, jagged and raw. I clutch at the sides of the wound trying to keep them closed, to keep my child safe. Fingertips bloody, I know, as a mother, I'm already failing.

In the crush, familiar and unfamiliar faces merge. The beat reverberates through the sprung floor. The crack in my side widening, my child shifts pressing against my insides, macerating them. Blood and fluid seep from me.

I'm handed shots— *Seven Deadly Sins and Baby Janes*— and down them. Droplets of grenadine soak into lace and meld with streaks of darker, congealed blood. With each gulp, I bury any thoughts of the harm they could do. I lean into the impulse to spin. Arms up, I move as concentrically as my uneven and swollen body allows.

11

When the pains come, I'm not surprised. My entire bump contracts and quivers. My skin pulling taut and then slack. My grunting lost under the '90s playlist we devised nights before. Around me, the celebrations continue undeterred.

In the crowd, I can't see my husband nor my mother, yet I'm glad. The room is muted. The waves of nausea, the pain, the blood and mess, and the baby, these are mine alone.

All at once, I'm present and I'm not. I'm hidden and then bathed in the strobes. As I moan, as flesh is cleaved, the smell of sweet, damp soil emanates from the widening spilt. The layers of dead leaves and earth that blanket my baby are exposed.

I let out long howls of shushing and panting as my bodice and skin give way like punctured orange peel. I'm softened, I am spilt open. I'm something new. My child is coming, and I wait to greet the creature I've created.

Teaching a Clean Front Kick

After my red belt ceremony, my sister asks me to train her. To defend against the bad guys. She kicks the air and swipes, a Mr Miyagi wax-on-wax-off move. Lack of discipline like hers is difficult to control.

When she was born, I tried to sit on her. Crush her tiny, baby bones. Alone in the lounge. I didn't put all my weight on her. Just enough. She was quiet at first, and then her muffled, fervent cry came through stronger. I felt her diaphragm sink and inflate. It was Uncle Jerry who pulled me from her. His tight grip on my wrist. His face all twisted up. I was usually the one invited to sit on his knee. The one he called his dumpling. But, from that moment, I understood she was his new favourite.

When she's finished flailing, I show her a Choku Zuki. A straight punch. Then, Mae Geri. A clean front kick.

"Draw back fully," I instruct. "That's where the power comes from."

When I explain about spiritual energy, she looks at me with burning intensity.

"Harness your mental strength," I say.

When she asks what I picture, I don't tell her that I visualise the pepper spray kept in my backpack or the way Mum taught me to clench my housekeys in my fist.

I don't tell her I think about the way Uncle Jerry says my name. Each syllable drawn out. Pausing so long, I pray the next sound won't come. But it does. The final vowel dripping from his mouth like treacle, like the thick, dark ooze of tar.

I don't say I think about the nights when Mum is downstairs dicing garlic and chives for gyozas, and Uncle Jerry moves quietly from my room into hers.

"Kick again," I say. "Harder."

Some Girls are Just Trashy and No Good

The funfair is our slice of Americana spread across the far playing field behind Marcie's house. Late August, we go the last night it's in town. We've seen *Grease* and understand all good things end with a flying car and a fairground. We're all about the lights, about toffee apples and green and blue candy floss. We're all about the hot oil and fried doughnuts. Our lips coated with vanilla sugar, we call to the Year Nine boys who smoke weed in the dark gap between the carousel and the funhouse, and we giggle when they yell back, "Alright, babe."

We play Hook-a-Duck and win reams of pink tickets, which we trail from the back pockets of our jean shorts or trade in for stuffed animals that we parade about with on our heads or draped around our shoulders like prized furs until we tire of carrying them and leave them where they fall.

We ride The Twister in pairs so that with each revolution we slide the length of the plastic seat. As the metal arms whirl us through space and time, our bony hips grind against the ride's outer-most point, and we

15

clasp the steel safety bar to save our bodies from slipping under and out completely.

Lights throb and we shriek and shriek above the music, we think about the force it takes to spin at such speed. We watch the pistons thumping in and out to move us to-and-fro and how this seems like sex, or what we think we know of it from biology lessons and TV shows: gyrating, moaning forms in dimly lit bedrooms and toilet cubicles. Our throats and cheeks flush pink as we imagine the warmth of our neon-stained mouths pressing against the ride attendant's ear, kissing his neck, and repeating his name as he speeds up The Twister to full throttle. He's somewhere around seventeen, milky skin and sandy hair, we call him, Danny or Kenickie, Raphael or Mikey, Donnie, or Leo. We don't care, but he's ours, until, still panting, we take the exit ramp.

We snake our way through the maze of mirrors laughing at how our foreheads are extended and our noses shrunk. But we spend the most time marvelling at how our curves could stretch and swell. Shaking our womanly butts backwards in the glass. Arching our backs and making baby bumps appear before squealing at the thought of it and making

16

our hasty getaway to the Dodgems, where we'll take no prisoners and drive headlong into everything.

Three rounds on the Waltzers and the boys track us down. They're silhouetted against a day-glow mural of John Travolta, Bart Simpson and the Hulk saying, "Smash!" Muddy kneed and bleary eyed they flock around us like gulls squawking for their prize, offering up sips of cider, and telling us we're beautiful. And, while the lights of the fair are dimming, some of us cry off, claiming missed curfews and queasy stomachs. While bold few, those not content that fantasy will sustain them until next time the fair rolls into town, tiptoe beyond the playing fields in search of something more, leaving the rest of us to wonder what will happen in the morning when the funfair has packed up and patches of faded, flattened grass are all that remain.

Adult Teeth

There's a tree in our yard that has teeth. No hinged jaw, just rows of molars and incisors pressed into its bark. Some are buried, a good swift hit with the mallet gets them in there tight. Some remain exposed. Sitting proud: bony nodules are all raised like braille.

My sister, Sissy, stands beside Mama and the tree with a newly excised tooth gripped in her palm. She shifts weight from foot to foot. Her wiry, adolescent limbs buzz with anticipation. Her cerise-painted lips freshly blotted, she's all too eager to be considered a woman in Mama's eyes.

Generations ago, our family had chosen the tallest, straightest tree. The one that didn't waver and whose roots anchored firm in the earth. We gift our baby teeth for luck and beauty, at least that's what Mama told us. But thinking about our cramped house with its leaking roof, cupboards bare of everything but gin, about the things we've had to do since Daddy left, about how each man seems more needy than the last, I wonder if Mama understands what luck or beauty mean at all.

I know which teeth are mine—the ones that seem larger and whiter than the older specimens that spiral the lower section of trunk. But Mama says mine are small and yellowed, that I should have taken more care to hit them in straight.

"Men don't want no crooked-toothed woman," warns Mama as Sissy strikes again at the cloudy crown of her last milk tooth.

Sissy has hammered every one of her teeth in with the same unwavering enthusiasm. She still believes every tale Mama has ever spun us, and today is no different. She gleams proudly at the tooth now firmly embedded in the tree's flesh, her smile showing almost all thirty-two of her new adult teeth. Mama coos at the sight. I stay quiet. Soon, Sissy will be expected to earn her keep just as I am.

~

That night, I take a man to bed, so Sissy doesn't have to.

I sit, one leg draped over the other just as Mama taught. Doe-eyed and quiet, I draw my lips into a smile exposing my gap-tooth, and the man reciprocates with his own rotten grin. With his whole weight on me, I picture the moon-licked tree, its leaves glossy, its trunk wide, studded like a pomander, fattened by my sister's newly gifted tooth.

Waiting for him to be done, I squeeze my eyes shut. I listen for Sissy in the bathroom flossing, brushing, rinsing, and spitting.

Perhaps she'll be lucky and marry quick like Mama wants.

Hidden in the Margins of a Gideon's Bible

The rollaway cot in the motel room is broken so my kid sister and I top
and tail next to Momma on the bed.

We take turns to check she's still breathing. Tenderised, fluid seeping
from her swollen-shut eye, her body reminds me of the joints of beef
she used to roast on Sundays.

Cupping tonight's dinner of Trail Mix and Cheetos in her palm, my
sister asks if he'll find us here. I don't answer but think about the pistol
nestled in the nightstand drawer, beside the bible, where *God help us* is
scrawled in Momma's scratchy, curving script.

Echoed Back

"They met on the toilet bowl when he was locked up."

My sister's high and giggling as she tells me this.

"Heads down their echoey, metal toilets they yelled to each other."

"How'd you know?"

"Hammer told me. It's a thing they do in prison."

We'd both known Hammer since we were kids. His parents lived on our block. I always saw through his over-shined Subaru with spoiler and tinted windows. His grin so wide you could easily slip inside. I always caught the sharp edges of his sleazeball routine, but Cassie kept a soft spot for him. He'd show up, croon *Mi Chica* and she'd crack open.

"She ain't on the scene no more?"

Cassie swigs at the whiskey and then passes it to me. She has that same look as her sixteen-year-old self, eyes wide and moony waiting out on our front porch with the fireflies and the promise of something more.

"She's still inside. Her head down the toilet chatting to some new guy," she tells me.

"That's some real shit," I say.

We laugh whiskey out our noses then. And I wonder if she'll tell me, it'll be different this time, that he's changed, that after all these years they've grown as people, you know. She doesn't. She leaves with him. Stumbles after him, ready to take his pills and the punches he offers up, the ones that when he gets a little heavy leave her with purple-stippled bruises and five cracked ribs.

~

In the morning, forehead pressed to the porcelain rim of the toilet bowl,

I imagine her honeyed voice drifting up through the sick and piss. I

imagine her coming down in another city, even another state by now. I

imagine Hammer's throaty Subaru speeding down an empty highway,

its paintwork slick in the hazy early morning sun. I squint through the

dark glass to see her eye socket etched with shadow, him pounding his

fist against steering wheel, her pleading with him to slow down before

they lose control completely. I imagine how things could've gone if I'd

done something more than laugh . . . but echoed up through the pipes

all I hear is *Chica, Chica, Chica.*

The Asarco Smokestack '93

The first time my sister talked about running away was when our stepmother gave us dolls' clothes she'd sewn from scraps of our mother's bath robe. When my sister had ripped them at their tiny seams and cried, Jane had called her ungrateful and said Dad should smack us, which he did. Sal had showed me the print his palm left on her flesh. She told me how she'd gone under the kitchen table and Jane had pulled her out by her ankle like a whippet snaring a rabbit.

~

The damp on our bedroom ceiling grows like soda poured too fast, bubbling up in patches. I tell my sister that the latest growth looks like her. She slaps me, pushing herself up from the bed next to mine and leaning close, but says I'll miss her when she's gone.

~

25

As we grow, Sal's plans become more elaborate. She'll go north of Tacoma to watch the towering smokestack that billows clouds of lead and copper into the sky. She'll travel to Europe, to The Sistine Chapel, so she can crane her neck to see Michelangelo's frescoes. She'll keep bees in the valley of Durance and grow lavender in endless domed rows of purple. At night, she sprawls herself across the globe. Running ever faster away from here until she's gone completely.

~

It's late and I don't know why I'm out in the bat-swooping twilight wearing only my night dress, turquoise fringing brushing my thighs, my toes dug deep into the stones, but I thought I heard Sal whispering to me. I'm standing beside the fence that divides our property with the next one. I'm on the gravel side where the cars park and our neighbour's son is in the paddock, the grass side, where the sheep graze. He's flicking a lighter. It's fizzing but not catching. I ask, and he hands it to me through the squares of wire. I flick the spark wheel with my thumb. It grinds, leaving pink ridges in my flesh. On the third spin, the blue-orange flame erupts. We share a cigarette and puff smoke out into the frigid night. He doesn't ask to come closer or touch me. I know, like me, he's wishing I was Sal.

~

When Sal has been gone a full month, I go to the gasoline station on the corner of our street. It's been repurposed as a religious centre for years now and the pumps on the old forecourt are painted with messages from God. During Sunday meetings, when most families were inside, Sally and I used to bike down together and take turns pretending to guzzle from the pump that said, "fill up with old time salvation and you will be reborn."

~

When Mom left, we watched from the window. The car was a muted, mossy green. The taillights glowed in the dark. The voices were muffled, but we knew it was bad. We understood tone by then. And, when Jane arrived, we watched from the window as she kissed Dad. Both of them pressed to the metal shell of his works van. Her arms

27

weren't around his neck; instead, she balanced her weight against the van, her fingers pushed into the groove of the door's sliding side panel.

~

On the nights when Dad and Jane take themselves upstairs, I tuck myself under the kitchen table until the floor joists stop creaking. It's not our kitchen table. It has rounded corners. It's baby blue, a colour my mother would never allow and is rimmed with metal. I trace the ridges where Sal carved her name into its underside years ago.

~

Waiting to collect my kids from the religious centre that's now a mixed martial arts gym, I'm older than Mom when she left, and younger than Jane when she died. One of the original gas pumps stands in the parking lot, the faded features of Jesus just visible. *Be sure to fill up with the Holy Ghost and fire.*

~

At home, I feed my hungry boys dinners of melanzane di parmigiana,

and desserts of shop-bought tiramisu. And after they're in bed, I stand

on our porch and smoke, thinking about Italy and France or that corner

of Tacoma and the smokestack they brought crashing down in 1993.

Practising Tricks, Spells, and Other Incantations

You're seven when I fracture my wrist, still young enough to believe in

magic. You buy a kilo of spinach from the grocery store with pennies

saved from mowing lawns. It's wilted and limp. (There's a variety

named *Black Magic*, but you couldn't find that.) You boil it in Gran's

cast iron pot, which you struggle to lift from the stovetop. You feed me

spoons of gleaming, emerald pulp that you're sure you've enchanted,

and stare at my limbs as if willing my brittle bones to mend with love

alone.

"Eat up, dear," you urge, your voice becoming the kindly Mrs Potts,

gentle and fragile like fine china.

Beauty and The Beast is your favourite film, the one we watch on

repeat when Mother's out practising tricks. You sob when Beast is

dying, but marvel at how he's transformed in the end. You're young

enough to believe there are such things as hope and redemption.

~

On nights Mother doesn't go out but brings her work home, we must stay quiet. She tells us the men are dangerous and wild. Fellow magicians you say, as you watch through a crack in our bedroom door, when Mother contorts them and makes them howl. Sometimes, you swear it's a body sawn in half, sometimes they're escaping from chains. Tonight, you whisper, "Levitation." Watching and waiting for a moment of wonder that doesn't come, I pull you away and into bed before mother has the chance to catch you spying.

~

The following day, when we're in town, mother yanks us away from an old woman ranting about creatures of the night with piercing teeth and rocket-shaped bodies that can tear through water and fire all the same, of beasts who stalk in the shadows, of sinners, and you strain against her grip to listen, hopeful that you'll hear her proclaim that with a touch of magic even the cruellest creatures are capable of change.

Loss Is Riding the Log Flume
at Splash Town in Late Summer

Katy Morris dares you to keep your hands high above your head as
you tip over the edge into watery oblivion. Loss is her laugh when you
refuse, hands still clamped to the safety bar.

Loss is the descent. It's steep. Foaming rapids soaking your shirt.
Katy's shape presses into you as the cart jolts back onto its rails. The
way she looks at you, damp hair, freckles glistening with spray. It
makes you jab your tongue to the roof of your mouth.

Loss is the candy floss you buy after. Its pink fluffiness. Wispy sugar
strands turned liquid by water in the air. Deep magenta syrup like your
first period that you won't experience for another year and a half.

Loss is the way Katy tells you her mother says to always carry pads in
your purse, in case she leaks through her drawstring shorts. She says
some girls have it tougher than others. It's the way she tells you it's not
all bad, before she leans in. Before she kisses you. Her lips sticky,
sugar, sweet.

Loss is entering the corn maze at full speed, hands entwined, running as one, past the ticket booth boy, yelling. Towering, golden stems whipping your bare legs and bronzed arms. A succession of lefts followed by a right.

Loss is how a low dipping sun casts the longest shadows.

Loss is all those summers later, in a field that isn't a maze, that doesn't even have corn in it, with Rob. He whispers into your face, brushes your hair from your eyes, and half limp he pushes himself inside you, so you feel kind of full and empty all at once.

Loss is how, if the field was sown with corn, it would flatten under the weight of your bodies.

Loss is Katy leaving for college years ago, travelling, diving headlong into life.

Loss is you watching Splash Town become a mall, become a parking lot, become an empty space in the town where you grew up.

What If We Breathed Through Our Skin?

When he's thirteen, my son, who has his father's strong jaw and the parts of me that matter, turns into a frog. It's his skin first. It sheds in large coin-sized discs. I pull off the bigger, dryer flakes and bathe the sores beneath. He's startled by the patches of green that radiate like sun on stained glass.

"Maybe I have to bury myself like an African bullfrog," he says.

I picture his body blanketed in the clay-rich soil of our garden, hidden in the damp earth. It is a mother's duty to shade her child from the midday sun. Days before, his father had reappeared and hopped over our circle of salt without complaint. He had promised he would see his boy, and I promised he would not.

"The males guard their tadpoles until they spawn," my son continues.

Our home is filled with amphibians, and he knows them all. Their shape and size, and the perfect ambient temperature for each. My boy is smart, but he understands little about the dangers a father can bring.

"Colour that bright. You're meant for the rainforest," I tell him.

With his newly lengthened tongue, he catches a housefly: curling the insect into the fleshy pocket of his cheek.

All is calm then, until his fingers and toes begin to web. He shows me the membrane that's formed between his digits, as he clutches crystals of tiger's-eye and serpentine for comfort.

"It's time for you to swim," I tell him.

At the pond's edge, he pauses before slipping in and under. For a moment, there's nothing but mirror stillness, and I pray he'll surface. But I needn't worry for he's silk in the water. Pondweed and murk yield to the strength of his long hind legs.

After this first dip, he submerges himself, daily, for hours at a time. And I scan the woods surrounding our cottage checking for any shadows.

His father returns one evening, drunk, as I knew he would. Tenderising the doorframe with his fists.

"I know you're there. You goddamned witch," he caws, as we hide.

I tell my son, "keep low," and he does, the only light—the iridescent haze of the terrariums—reflecting in his golden, domed irises. Cowed on the rug, he seems smaller than ever. I have cuttings of borage, sage and wormwood, but they aren't enough. The shouting continues.

I begin to chant, and the glass tanks rattle. The frogs chirp and yammer. My son places his hands against the space where his ears once were, and I watch as parts of him contract and distort like stop motion. Yet, the thing I dreaded, his bones cracking, is tiny: fractures blooming on an eggshell before the bones reknit. They crumble, shrink, and reform.

"You are so beautiful, my boy," I say, when it's done. His skin, now free of its scabs, is slick and smooth. His body marbled with green so perfect he could be carved from jade.

The God, the Baby, and the Lichtenberg Figure

The electricity once shared with her husband has long since faded, yet

she aches. Unsure if it's the coldness of their bed or her empty womb,

she creeps outside. The thrum of the storm promises something new.

In the fields, she finds his silhouette etched on the towering corn,

Mjölnir held aloft. Surrendering herself, tributaries of purple perforate

the sky. The anvil cloud above them swells.

She steadies her nerve and the lightning crackles. Lichtenberg figures

plume across her skin. Body humming, she kneels in the dust and waits

until he grants her rain heavy enough to nourish new life.

How to Bake Cookies
When Your Child is Dying

1) Wait until the house is sleeping and you're alone. Leave your husband's side and creep into the kitchen.

2) Weigh out each ingredient into separate bowls; line them up on the countertop and tell yourself you're regaining control.

3) Cream the butter and sugar together (by hand, as the stand mixer would wake your husband and children). Beat until smooth, beat until the ache in you forearm is deep enough to get lost in. Until you stop listening for the rhythm of breaths from the bedroom above. Pacing out the gap between each one. Waiting out the pause the same way you used to count the seconds between each thunderclap as a child.

4) As you combine the eggs, slowly, willing them not to curdle, don't think about hospital beds and beeping machines that whir and slosh, cleaning blood when the kidneys have all but been eaten away and can no longer function as they should. Don't think about the look on your

40

husband's face as he said that it might not get that far and squeezed your hand.

5) Try to swirl in some of your daughter's boundless hope and strength with a cupful of chocolate chunks and two tablespoons of peanut butter. Mimicking the flavours of her favourite candy seems like a meaningless gesture, but what else can you do?

6) Sift in the flour. Hold the sieve high and gently tap the rim. You want to get as much air into the mix as possible. Imagine a sense of weightlessness. Let the pressure of telling her dissipate. Breathe out the heavy panic that masses within you, your stomach full of gravel when you think about how to explain words like leukaemia, metastasis and malignant.

Note: If the flour plumes about you, let it. Allow it to coat the shoulders of your nightshirt. Hold your palms up, so it settles in the creases of your skin. Catch the fine dust of it like dandelion fluff blown to you by your daughter's strong, even breaths. Eyes shut, dance in honeyed, knee-high meadow-grass and let yourself see the sun. If only for a

moment.

7) Use a figure-eight method to fold in the flour. Slowly, like your
mother taught you. Steady, fluid twists doubling back and back. Feel
the rhythm of it. The firmness of her grip on yours. A firmness that she
never wavered from, a firmness that made her tough, that kept her
knees from buckling when she lost the three babes after you, when her
full-grown son died in a far-off corner of the earth, when Papa passed,
and she chastised your tears as weakness. If the mixture is too wet, add
more flour as needed and consider how to retain resilience without
growing scornful and cold.

8) Bake. Get down on your knees and move close enough so the warm,
orange glow of the oven bathes your face as you watch balls of dough
dome up, and let yourself cry when they sink back down, and form a
crust that only reminds you of displaced earth, the slowly collapsing
mound of a freshly backfilled grave.

The Manicure

I peed with the toilet door open. No need for formalities: motherhood had relaxed me that way. I didn't even have makeup on. She eyed me from her perch on our bed, feet dangling. I'm not Grace's mother in the traditional sense, not by blood, but she is mine. She doesn't know anything different. She's eight and a half.

"Don't touch." I said, "They'll be tacky."

"Tacky?"

I was shocked by the words she'd yet to learn and wondered whether teacher was in my remit.

"Still sticky," I said. I stood up, shook, and wiped. I figured it was healthy for her to see the matured female form. I went to the sink and opened the hot tap full. My skin was sepia in the bathroom light. Grace was too young to care how I looked.

She'd begged for a manicure for weeks. Molly goes to the salon with her mum and gets a cola, and little diamonds glued on.

I'd protested, but she hadn't let it drop. Each night, after school, she'd stare at her bare nails and sigh. On the seventh day, I finally relented and picked a bottle of bubble-gum sparkle from my collection. I'd vetoed the slutty shade of crimson that she'd chosen.

Coming out of the bathroom, Grace was pecking at the packet of cookies I'd bought.

I found the red plastic tab and unfurled the biscuits, triumphantly. I held one above her mouth. She guzzled it in three handless bites, and then smiled, lips ringed with crumbs.

For the film, we'd chosen *Freaky Friday*, the original version. Lindsay Lohan was a step too far for me. I slid the DVD in, and she pressed play with her elbow.

"Ready for the topcoat?" I asked.

She gave me her hands. Her spindle-thin wrist felt dependent in my

grip. Her tiny nails only needed the smallest daub of polish.

A young Jodie Foster and her mother, a long dead actress whose name I

can't remember, yelled at each other. I could tell Grace wasn't sure –

the colour wasn't crisp enough, and the phones had cords. Another

mother might have picked something cooler. There was something

about the way she was sitting: one leg draped over the other, chest all

puffed out like a pintsized pinup. She was only enduring this to humour

me.

Once she had her glittering nails, I studied her shape; over the past few

years, she'd shed her girly plumpness, but not yet gained curves. The

first time I saw her, she was so small, not quite six months old. Her

skin had seemed almost transparent. Blue-purple veins just visible

beneath a soft, pinkish top layer. She was a featherless chick in my

arms mewing and squawking for nourishment. It was the first time I'd

ever held something so fragile.

45

On the screen, Jodie Foster flickered, her silhouette glowed orange and then green. Mother and daughter echoed the same words, and for a moment, Grace was interested. There was a flash of light that indicated the swap had happened. Grace laughed, and I tried to imagine her becoming me. Not in an instant, but slowly over sometime. Her face morphing to match mine: her body filling out. I pictured her in a pair of my patent heels, kissing boys with cherry-glossed lips. I saw her naked in a man's bed, his hands tracing this new body's form. I watched her innocence seep away as she stole another woman's husband, and I felt thankful her face could never actually resemble mine.

The Difference Between Love and Plant Life

Jon and I met six months ago on a dating website, his profile photo: him felling a tree, mid-swing. His occupation: landscape gardener. I clicked match.

When I visit my mother to tell her I'm engaged, we sit and drink tea on her patio. I can still sense the space between us as dense and sharp as gorse.

"I'm glad you've found someone who can sooth you," Mum says. "You've always been skittish. Even as a child you could never be still. Like you were always being chased."

I think about a day when I was five. The first time I remember running from anything. We'd been at the park since lunch. Dad away on a work trip. I saw Mum with a man who wasn't my father.

She got into a car the colour of a Venus flytrap. Slick green outside. Red leather seats inside: a cherry-red throat. It was a convertible, a

Cadillac. The engine was deep and raw. Nothing like our family people carrier.

The man in the driver's seat gripped Mum's wrist and moved close to her ear. Their mouths pushed together. His slick, pink tongue visible for a second. Darting about and then retracting, disappearing. Mum gasping for breath. His head at her neck, and then dipping lower out of sight. Their movement reminded me of vines, the creeping type I'd seen on TV. Writhing, growing and wrapping around someone's ankle before ripping them away to some place dark. I wanted to shout out then or run to her and beat my fist against the door. My breath loud in my ears as the vines coiled tighter.

~

"Jon could sort the garden for you, Mum," I say.

Amongst the weeds swelling around us, Mum pours more tea. The slabs of the patio have warped; the sand foundations are weak after years of rain. The whole area needs repointing.

"The garden was always more your father's domain," Mum says, waving the suggestion away.

"He's a good guy. You'll like Jon," I tell her.

Jon is rugged. His skin has the warmth of Redwood bark. He is tall and strides with purpose. And I like that with every deliberate step he sends out a network of roots that lend him unrivalled stability. When we are intimate, he holds my face in his rough palms so I can study the green that stains his fingertips.

Mum says nothing, and I feel the carpet of undergrowth around us inch closer.

~

It was only after Dad died that Mum reached out and asked me to come home. I was twenty-five. I handled all the funeral arrangements alone while Mum ate the many condolence meals delivered by her

49

neighbours and struggled with anything more than two syllables. And after the service, while Mum grieved, I hooked up with the catering manager in the downstairs cloakroom. His dick was as soft as fresh bamboo and afterwards, I cried as the vines snaked under the locked door.

This was not unlike my first time, when Benjamin Harris had told me I was beautiful over and over until he came. We had lain on the crusted mud behind the bike shed. And I'd wanted to believe him. I'd wanted him to cradle me like a seedpod, but he rolled away, so when I closed my eyes all I saw was the lime Cadillac and the vines.

In college, a guy from my study group, who had a thing for vintage movies, made me watch *The Day of the Triffids*. He liked the kitchen sink special effects: the tin foil and painted papier mâché. Having sex, we let the film play. Half the world blinded, and I was transfixed by the triffids' greenness, their spiny, mauve thistle heads, their gnashing teeth stacked up in rows, circular like a shark's. Watching them feast, I was that girl again flung back to the park, not understanding, the desire and shame bubbled within me.

50

~

The heat of the garden is dry and suffocating. The shrubs that surround us are yellowing. And the blackberry bush, with its mass of thorny, interweaving stems, is heavy with oily black fruits. When Jon arrives, I let him in the side gate. He hugs me, and I inhale his earthy scent of grass mulch. I marvel at how he picks handfuls of berries without a scratch.

Behind us, Mum is in the centre of a growing briar patch. Stems of hawthorn pulse, and I think of my fear nurtured from seed. I hear her voice echoing from the past.

"When I tell you to stay, you stay, you hear?"

When she'd found me, I'd clung to her then as I bind to Jon now. I pull Jon's hands, so they cover my ears, blocking out Mum's thirty years of chastising. Vines spiral at our feet, and at hers. Lashing to our legs, sprawling, woody creepers threaten to envelop us like always.

51

I daren't breathe.

I shudder as their tendrils braid tighter around my ankles, feeling them squeeze and tug.

But Jon's roots hold fast, firm, and steady, just as I hoped they would.

The Secret to a Maze is to Keep Turning Left

The corn is at its tallest where we enter.

Buttery silk tassels catch in our curls. Arms outstretched, we twist off

the lower leaves as we

run,

      leaving them

            scattered in

                  our wake: breadcrumbs for anyone bold

            enough to follow.

Our footfalls echo over sun-baked ground. We're abuzz for boys

wearing cut-off shorts and for stolen cigarettes we're too chicken to try.

Come September, on opposite sides of the county, we'll pin up

identical Polaroids, XOXO inked in their frames, our closeness a

glossy, laminated memory. Spiralling towards the centre, we race to

outrun the shadows at summer's end.

The Space Between Where We've Been and Where We Are is Saltwater

Friends suggested floatation therapy when Steve left. Reborn was the word they used.

She fills their tub with Epsom salts and runs the tap. With magnesium sulphate, a foot of water is all that's needed. She lets the crystals dissolve. Draping towels across the bath, she cocoons herself in the dark.

At first, she rages against the confines of the tub, against his starched shirts, lost mixtapes, and ticket stubs, smiling portraits, cheap Greek holidays, and cancer scares, his and hers, until, lulled by the water's stillness, she floats.

The click of the fridge motor echoes through the floorboards from the kitchen and, as she listens to sounds reverberate through their empty house, her brain starts to hum at a new frequency. Her weightless limbs create only the slightest of ripples in the water before the sides of the tub give way.

She's at a lake's edge, perhaps the lake that backed onto her grandmother's cabin, perhaps Lake Ontario, where she and Steve had rented a cottage for the summer, or perhaps even the banks of Loch Morar, where she had tried to numb her grief with the cold.

Both moving and still, she paddles in a brook, she sits on the broad bed of a braided stream and sinks into the silt. Standing on the stony bottom, she slips, searches the contours of slick, cool rocks for a foot hold.

She wades in. Ankle to thigh, abdomen to breasts. Faced with the expanse of a frigid loch, she listens as mist whispers across its surface willing her under. Daring her to consider the child that never really got to be theirs—hers.

She plunges deep. Pushing hard against the burning of her lungs, she dives down, but she's surprised by how much see wants to keep breathing. How much her body flights to stay afloat. So, she allows herself to rise.

For a moment nothing happens, and then she is buoyant again, her body

bobbing to the surface like a lobster buoy signalling the presence of full

pots below. She waits for her mind to catch up, taking one slow breath

and then another until letting go feels natural and she's certain that

when she emerges from the tub, finally—sloughing salty skin—she'll

feel somehow lighter.

Moon Swimming and Monster Hunting

With mother already swallowed by the sea, and father swallowed by the bottle, his evenings nursing beer after beer, we slip out unnoticed and seek our freedom on the beach. In the shallows, we bob and float uninhibited, listening to the sound of the ocean sucking against the shore.

The water is oil-slick in the moonlight. Our bodies curved, our knees pulled tight to our chests, we practice mushrooms floats in the water. Rocked by the current, our pale backs crest out from the waves. We imagine ourselves as beluga whales with ethereal, white heads. Magical and strange. The kind of creature you'd see etched at the edge of ancient, pirate maps.

Whenever we find the courage to ask father about mother, the rare occasions he's home with us, his funds for drink run dry, he tells us she's a siren or he calls her a Selkie. Freddie says that's why we come to the beach and why we feel at home in the water. We've been told about the dangers, about creatures that lurk beneath the surface, but being children, we've spent hours combing rock pools for mermaids'

purses as proof our mother remains hidden somewhere in the depths.

Sometimes, I picture mother as a figurehead. Her face carved into a

pirate ship's prow guiding them towards treasure, whereas Freddie

likes to call to her. His holler's stretching as far as the inky horizon. He

waits, treading water, but most of the time only his voice is echoed in

return.

Tonight, it's much the same as his shouts trail back to us, but

something's different. The pattern of ripples in the water suggests

we're not alone. And sure enough, in front of us, those ripples soon

become a whirlpool out of which a figure emerges. Their body fringed

with ribbons of seaweed; their face framed by deep-set gills, they're

nothing like I imagined my mother would be, no sweeping fish tail,

golden with scales, but their eyes are wide and dark. Filled with the

unknown possibility of deep water, they shimmer in the moonlight like

ours. And when the figure beckons, Freddie ducks under the waves first

and then, I follow.

The Depth at Which Spider Crabs are Found

Each weekend, Mother would cook while Dad dove for baskets of spiny spider crabs hauled up from the seafloor. Until one afternoon, he failed to surface.

We paced the beach and shouted his name into the mean expanse of ocean that stretched beyond the horizon. I wanted to take a boat and search the waves, but Grandpa told us he knew the kraken had stolen my father away.

Mother said that this was just folklore. A whisper of something lost. The seafarer's nightmare. Yet as I grew, I found bones washed up on the shore. Vertebras hiding among sea glass, polished smooth. A thigh bone as bleached and gnarled as driftwood. A mandible stripped of all its flesh and teeth.

At twelve, I learnt to dive too. Taking the scavenged bones with me, hooked to my suit, I learnt to navigate the current, gage the pressure of each new depth and maintain buoyance. I learnt to push deeper, search for all things hidden, and pluck only the sweetest, plumpest crabs.

And at twenty-five, the creature was there to greet me, its beaked mouth wide. Splayed, ruptured like the figs mother used to bake. Purple flesh peeled back into a gruesome smile. Fig seeds exchanged for razor edged teeth.

Thorns Are Meant to Prick the Heart of Sinners

The roses became a fixture after Daddy disappeared. Scathing late night whispers exchanged for endless digging, planting and pruning.

And now, the stench of boiling bones seeps into every pore of our house but it's thickest in the kitchen, where mother has three pots bubbling away for bonemeal. Sweet, sickly steam rises and clings to the ceiling.

At her feet, there's a fresh thicket of roses she's yet to plant. Roots submerged in water, a thorny crown of stems twists upwards. She steps over them to greet me before she drifts back to her roses, back to the bones she'll cook until almost jelly. The bones that, once dried out, she'll grind to powder.

~

The following day, she moves from bones to wilted blooms for rosewater, which she'll wear daubed on her wrists and neck.

61

Scent bottles with ornate stoppers join the jars of fresh bone dust on the countertop. The ground bone separates into layers of ochre and grey and at the bottom, where larger shards have settled, there's a glimmer of something else. I reshuffle them as I watch her, twisting the jars this way and that so the metallic flecks catch the light like Daddy's polished class ring.

I want to ask about Daddy. If he's lost and can't find his way home. If he's with that woman from his work, Marline, who mother says is too old to wear cherry brandy coloured lipstick and skirts that hug her hips.

Instead, I say, "The oldest living rose is a thousand years old."

She won't look at me because I have Daddy's features, his sharp chin, his high cheek bones.

"It's at Hildesheim Cathedral in Germany." I continue, but her gaze stays firmly fixed on the mass of congealed petals in front of her. And I wonder what it is that the roses say to her. What they whisper; what they offer her as she sings to them. What secrets they keep hidden? What it takes to keep living for a thousand years?

"Imagine that," I say.

~

That evening, I take a jar of bonemeal from the kitchen and follow mother into the garden. She digs with her hands like an animal, and with fingers scratching in the earth, she buries the millipede roots of a Black Baccara. Then a sprawling, spiny dog rose whose barbs are dense and needle sharp.

I cough to announce my presence, but Mother focuses on coaxing unruly petioles around a half-rotten length of trellis.

"Where is he?" I ask, hugging the jar to my chest.

She works faster then, arching stems and coiling them tight against the latticework. Thorns lacerating her hands and arms, I watch her skin turning red.

"Tell me."

She opens her mouth to speak, and I sigh imagining that she'll tell me he'll be back soon with candies and a dozen sweetheart roses wrapped in tissue paper. And that I'd be shocked by any other answer.

"He's likely just cooling off somewhere," she says, finally.

~

When I raise the jar above my head, Mother's mouth is a perfect, gaping oval. Dropped, glass fizzes like fireworks and gritty plumes of bonemeal choke the air. Mother clamps her hands across her mouth and nose so that she doesn't inhale the particles of Daddy and Marline that swirl around us.

When I tilt my head skywards and stick out my tongue, Mother's eyes widen.

Awaiting the taste of iron and dirt, thorns rupture along my spine and dusky, cherry brandy buds blossom from my throat. I'm the Hildesheim rose that still clings to crumbling cathedral walls.

And Mother knows her fate is set.

The Locked Cupboard

At thirty-five weeks, when the life inside me is roughly the size of a honeydew melon, my mother arrives with a chicken-arugula salad.

In the living room, a damp washcloth spread across my swollen belly, I place an ice cube under my tongue. The numb ache is refreshing. My screen door is open, and from my place on the couch, I can see children having a water fight in the parking lot.

They hoard balloons of different sizes in large Tupperware dishes. A balloon ruptures on someone's windshield and my baby kicks. The counter barrage is launched releasing a slick of water onto the parched concrete.

While the fight rumbles on in the summer warmth, Mum tells me, "It's packed with prenatal nutrients." A phrase she's lifted from a new-age motherhood blog. Trying her best to ignore the neighbourhood kids' noisy joy, she puts the salad away in the refrigerator.

She's always taken it upon herself to regulate my food. When I was younger, we were only allowed all-bran cereal, the kind that keeps you regular, and the kitchen cupboards were locked.

"Rachel swore by avocados," I say. "I heard they're full of folate and vitamin B6, which promotes healthy tissue and brain growth for the baby."

My sister, Rachel, city slicker turned yogi, has always had what my mother terms lean and shapely calves. When pregnant, she commissioned a set of photos in monochrome: her, draped in soft tulle, and her husband's head, pressed against the bump.

Mum smiles. "It's probably time you started listening to your sister. She's always been the smart one. Her Larry's such a good provider. He's reliable. That's what you need in this life."

I don't say that Larry's boring. That he's the kind of man who believes you can only wear brown shoes with a grey suit and housework is divided simply into pink and blue jobs.

"He's a good father too. . .And when do we get to know anything about this baby's father?" she says, gesturing towards my stomach.

Outside, a child steps through the yellow, crisp grass. I wring out the washcloth and let droplets of water pool around my distended navel.

I selected the father for what the clinic cited as strong moral fibre. In the picture attached to his file, he was smiling widely in that uninhibited way kids often do. He's Canadian and I'm sure he wears plaid shirts on lazy Sundays. And the audio recording of his voice was smoother and more comforting than any physical guy I'd been with.

My mother knows about my decision to conceive this way but refuses to let it be, and the lack of patriarchal role model is a topic we've been circling since my first trimester.

"I'm everything my baby needs," I tell her.

"I just think . . . have you really thought this through . . . children need—"

"I am everything my baby needs."

Mum opens her mouth to speak but closes it again.

"Everything," I repeat. Slightly surprised by my unspooling intensity, I decide not to remind her that Dad left before Rachel and I were even ten.

In the fifteen or so seconds of silence that come next, Mum's jaw tightens and her shoulders sag, and I wonder if she's back there anyway, in those nights after Dad, when her sobbing was muted only by the double thickness plywood of her bedroom door. This was the only time I've thought of her as something fragile.

"It's beyond hot in here," she announces, finally. "Staying hydrated? And I bet you haven't been practising your antenatal breathing either."

She hands me another ice cube. I chew it this time, savouring the sting in my teeth.

"And those children out there. What a ruckus. I can't stand it."

I picture the smallest boy in the group, sandy haired and sunburnt. He's gap-toothed, like me at his age. If he were mine, I'd call him Kiddo, and ruffle his mop-top hair with my palm like they do in films. I'd tell him, throw another balloon. Pitch it skyward. Watch it soar. I'd say: I'm here for you. Aim high.

"That could be your grandchild," I say.

"Those terrors? This is what happens these days when women choose a man based on some well-written paperwork."

I don't reply, but instead, I breathe deeply releasing a practiced hee-hee noise, as I exhale.

Sometimes, I do wonder if my baby will have this stranger's face, his father's face, or my own. His nose or eyes, and my mouth. Sometimes, I think about travelling to Canada, when my boy is grown, and meeting this man. Hugging him and saying thank you. But for now, I'm just happy that this child is surviving and growing strong because of me.

~

Before she leaves, Mum asks if I want anything, and I tell her no. Reaching out, I touch her shoulder, goodbye. She steps back slightly and then relaxes letting my hand rest there for a moment, before telling me not to waste her salad.

Friday Night at the Cinema

They were at the cinema, my mum and her first boyfriend after my dad. They went to the last screening of *Pulp Fiction*. My dad followed them there: the headlights of his car on full-beam blinking in the rearview mirror. He turned left when they turned right. He took the second exit off the roundabout and doubled back. They were sure he'd gone. I can see the whole scene. The foyer has spotlights on and smells like sweet toast. Mum presses her hands to the glass of the popcorn warmer while her boyfriend collects the tickets. The lights are too bright. The image in my head is like a grainy television set.

This is not my own memory. It's my mum's, but it's like I inherited it. I nurtured it. She only ever told me one thing about it, in anger. I didn't appreciate what she'd been through bringing me up.

Although this is a stolen memory, I know it. I can see it as if it were mine; I'm close to it. I'm not looking in through binoculars.

She told me about the knife (a Swiss army penknife bought as a birthday gift by my grandparents) and how it was pressed into the back of the folding seat chair. I added the sound of ripping fabric. I can inhabit the space where it happened. The snap, snap of synthetic threads.

On the screen, John Travolta and Uma Thurman dance on an oversized clock face in monochrome outfits. They sweep their fingers over their eyes in a V-shape. Then they do that underwater jive thing. Clubbers watch them in a semicircle. Coloured lights flash. The wall behind the dance floor is stone effect.

I tried putting this memory alongside Bret's interrogation scene—Samuel L. Jackson shooting the couch—but it doesn't seem right. I think of the fan T-shirts that copy that image. The block-print. The moustache and Afro combo. I have watched the film ten times or more and I think all of this must have happened after the dance contest. It fits best alongside the bit with the adrenaline shot. Panic and then the loud intake of breath.

The problem is the event has become the movie. All Hollywood, a shiny wrapped package, unreachable. One of those parts in an action film where the good guy rolls from the shell of a burning car moments before it spontaneously explodes. He is unharmed and you find yourself saying "as if."

The lights are down, and the cinema is half-empty; that's how it happened, unnoticed.

My mum watches the screen. Her boyfriend's arm grazes her breast as he reaches for popcorn. She wriggles in her seat. Her boyfriend pauses, his hand halfway towards his mouth. He emits a squeal that is more like the sound of breath being stopped. His body is rigid. He tries to signal my mum with his eyes. His pupils move from side to side, the pressure from the knife in the small of his back, the tip of its blade dulled by the seat's padding.

My dad whispers: "Do you feel lucky, Punk." This isn't a question.

He has been sitting behind them the whole time. In fact, he was there first. This is how I see it. He wears ripped chinos and a jumper over a hooded top. The hood is up and shadows his eyes. His beard is unkempt.

Floatation Therapy

What if I could hold my breath long enough to dive the depths of a

murky ocean, could submerge myself and marvel at the softness of my

skin under the water, the way my limbs feel larger yet somehow

ethereal and light, before sinking deeper, traveling through each layer,

past the midnight zone, leaving angler fish blinking in the dark, where I

could refuse to be crushed by pressure mounting in my body, or what if

my diaphragm didn't need to inflate, what if I didn't need to

concentrate on my ragged breath, the sound of it caught in my chest

while I have sex with my best friend's guy (the one that works at The

Sub Shop, doling out warm, moist, sliced meats that look as appetizing

as a blob fish,) what if I didn't have to suck air into weak lungs and

pant and rasp like a deflating balloon animal before he came, what if I

were alone in my flat, save the one scorched and wilting cheese plant,

what if when the guy—my best friend's man—leaves, after wiping

himself on my hand towel, the one with the appliqued, silk starfish, the

one Mum bought as a housewarming gift, our family's only tradition,

everything could be calm and still, what if, once he was gone, I didn't

have to feel my body expand as I buried my face in the pillows letting out big, heaving sobs, what if instead of diving, running the risk of

decompression sickness, of gas bubbles forming in the circulatory

system, I could remain on the surface, face up, floating and weightless.

Acknowledgements

To my husband, Andy, thank you for your unwavering love and support. For all the cups of tea that made writing these stories that bit more achievable. Thank you for believing in me and putting up with my creative outbursts. Thank you to all my writerly friends for their continued positivity, kindness, and generosity, with special thanks to Genevieve Allen and Cecilia Kennedy for being first readers on most of these stories and always giving fantastic feedback. Thank you to everyone who has had a hand in this collection in some way. Thank you to the magazines and journals who like my stories enough to publish them. Thank you to my family and my *Flash Fiction Magazine* family. Thank you to anyone who reads, enjoys, and champions my writing. Thank you to *Dialect*'s mentorship for giving me the opportunity to be mentored by Mahsuda Snaith, which in turn gave me the courage to send my words into the world as a collection. Thank you to my very first mentor, D.D. Johnston, who helped me earn my MA and taught me so much about writing good stories.

To my blurbers: Laura Besley, Amy Cipolla Barnes, and Liza Olson—the biggest of thank yous for your thoughtful words about my words and the time you took writing them.

And finally, thank you to Red and *Alien Buddha Press* for believing in and creating this book.

About the Author

Keely O'Shaughnessy is a fiction writer with cerebral palsy, who lives in Gloucestershire, U.K. with her husband and two cats. She has been shortlisted for the Bath Flash Fiction Award and won *Retreat West*'s Monthly Micro contest. Her micro-chapbook, *The Swell of Seafoam,* was published as part of *Ghost City Press*' Summer Series 2022. Her writing has been published by *Ellipsis Zine, Complete Sentence, Reflex Fiction and Emerge Literary Journal, and (mac)ro(mic),* and more. Her short fiction has been nominated for the Pushcart Prize and Best Small Fictions as well as being selected for the Wigleaf Top 50. She is Managing Editor at *Flash Fiction Magazine.* Find her at keelyoshaughnessy.com

Printed in Great Britain
by Amazon

83499054R00048